More Spaghetti, I Say!

by
Rita Golden Gelman

Pictures by Jack Kent

SCHOLASTIC INC.
New York Toronto London Auckland Sydney Tokyo

For Jan and Mitchell

ISBN 0-590-02372-1

Text copyright © 1977 by Rita Golden Gelman. Illustrations copyright © 1977 by Jack Kent. All rights reserved. Published by Scholastic Inc.

20 19 18 17 16 15 14 13 12 11   4 5 6 7 8/8

Printed in the U.S.A.   07

"Play with me, Minnie.

Play with me, please.

We can stand on our heads.

We can hang by our knees."

"Oh, no.

I can't play.

I can't play with you, Freddy.

4

Not now.

Can't you see?

I am eating spaghetti."

"Now you can do it.
Now you can play.

We can jump on the bed
for the rest of the day."

"No. I can **not**.

I can **not** jump and play.

Can't you see?

I need more.

More spaghetti, I say!

I love it.
I love it.
I love it.
I do.

I love it so much!"

"More than me?"

"More than you."

"I love it on pancakes

with ice cream and ham.

With pickles and cookies,

bananas and jam.

I love it with mustard
and marshmallow stuff.

I eat it all day.
I just can't get enough.

I eat it on trucks,

and I eat it in trees.''

"You eat it too much.

Won't you play with me,

PLEASE?"

"I can run in spaghetti.

And ride in spaghetti.

I can jump.

I can slide.

I can hide in spaghetti.

I can skate on spaghetti,

and ski on spaghetti.

And look at this picture.

That's **me** on spaghetti."

"Spaghetti. Spaghetti.

That's all you can say.

I am going to throw your spaghetti away.

22

I am going to throw it all over the bed,

in the grass,

in the mud,

in the paint,

ON YOUR HEAD!"

"Oh, Minnie,
that look on your face!
You look bad.

You look big.
You look green.
You look sick.
You look sad."

"You are right.

I am green.

I feel sick.

Yes, I do.

I think I will rest.

I will sit here with you."

26

"Let me take this away now.
I think that I should.

And then we can play.

Mmmmmmmm! Spaghetti is good.

I love it.

I love it.

I love it.

I do.

I need more spaghetti.

I can't play with you."

"But now I can play.

I can play with you, Freddy."

"Not now.

Can't you see?

I am eating spaghetti."